Monty
and the
Poppit Dragon

Cookie

Monty

To, Anna
Love from
Monty & Cookie

Story by M.T. Sanders
Illustrations by Zoe Saunders

First Edition published 2018 by 2QT Limited (Publishing)
Settle, NorthYorkshire BD24 9RH United Kingdom

Illustrations by Zoe Saunders

Printed in Great Britain by IngramSparks

A CIP catalogue record for this book is available from the British Library

ISBN 978-1-912014-06-4

Dedications

Mark - For all of our friends, followers and fans. Your support has been colossal and we can't thank you enough. You've enabled us to fly.

Monty - For Isla smiler and her amazing family and friends. Not many people can make the world a better place. You have x.

Zoe - For George and Matilda. May you grow up to be courageous, hopeful and resilient, just like the sweet Poppit Dragon. Let nothing hold you back. Find your wings and fly.

The story of the Slobbernosserus had been forgotten and Cookie was being slightly better behaved - well, most of the time.

Life was kind of normal and then one day Mum said, 'We're going to Wales on holiday.'

Bailey Spangle thought going to Wales meant we'd be spending a week on a big fish.

I told him Wales was a place and the Spangles could run around on the beach, and he seemed happy about that.

When we arrived, we all went off to explore and that meant a trip to the beach.

The Spangles went with Dad to chase the ball... then bring it back... then chase the ball... then bring it back.

I've never understood why the hoomans throw the ball if they want it back so badly.

Cookie and I went to the other end of the beach. All of a sudden, she ran off and disappeared into a cave.

I followed because I was sure she'd get into trouble - and that usually meant trouble for me, too.

She had disappeared to the back of the cave where it was dark.

All of a sudden I heard a crash and a loud... OUCH!

I was imagining all sorts of things that could have happened but nothing prepared me for what I saw next.

Cookie came slowly out of the darkness looking a little nervous.

Just behind her shuffled a very large, very red, very sad looking... What was that?

It looked like a- like a- a dr- a dra- a dragon!

But I'd seen them in books and they were meant to be scarier than this one.

It just stood sobbing beside Cookie. I can only imagine that my hairy sister had trodden on its foot because that's what I usually do when she treads on me.

'I'm sorry for my sister,' I said. 'Did she hurt your toe, er - claw - thingy?'

'No,' came the reply. 'I'm just sad. She didn't hurt me.'

'Oh okay, that's good... Come on, Cookie, we need to get back NOW. Bye.'

Cookie didn't come though. Instead she turned to the beast and said, 'Why are you sad?'

'We shouldn't bother her, Cookie,' I said. 'We really should be going. She probably has lots to do... fire breathing and maybe eating intruders.'

This just made the dragon sob louder. Cookie gave me one of those looks that usually come just before she leaps on me.

'Please don't be sad,' she said. 'My brother is always grumpy. He doesn't mean it.

I'm Cookie and this is Monty and we are on holiday. We can be friends, if you'd like.'

'I'd like that,' said the dragon.

'My name is Dilys and I'm the Poppit Dragon and I'm sad because I can't fly.

My brother and sister have already flown off to their dragon jobs but I was born with these tiny wings and big floppy ears, so I have to stay hidden in this cave. Oh, and in case you're worried, I can't do the fire breathing either.'

Well, Cookie and I just looked at each other. Before I could say another word, she blurted out, 'That's okay, we can help you fly. Monty is very clever and knows lots about everything. I'm sure we can get you in the air in no time - can't we, Monty?'

'Oh, would you?' cried Dilys excitedly, and her tears were replaced by a hooge dragon smile.

What could I do? She seemed so happy. But help a dragon fly? I was a Newfydoof and I even found swimming tiring. But then I thought of something. Why not ask the creatures that could fly how they did it? Then I was sure Dilys would soon learn and we could get back home for our dinner.

Off we went, two Newfydoofs and a dragon, in search of the answer. It wasn't long before we came across a seagull perched on top of a sand dune. I introduced us and told the seagull why we were there. Could he teach Dilys how to fly?

'I'm Steven Seagull,' he said in a squawky voice.

The seagull soars with mighty wings.
You'll surely fail with those tiny things
You asked my advice and I can't lie
I don't think that you will ever fly.'

With that, he leapt off the sand dune and flew
gracefully away across the sea.

Dilys looked sad again so I said quickly, 'Give it go, Dilys. It doesn't look too hard.'

She got into position nervously and, with a leap, she...

...faceplanted in the sand, leaving the biggest dragon-shaped hole you've ever seen.

Before she had time to get upset again, we headed off. Before long, we came across an owl sitting high up in a tree.

'Hello, Owl,' I said. 'My name is Monty and my friend here, Dilys, would like some tips on flying. Mind if she joins you up there?'

'I'm Olivia Owl,' she hooted.

'On silent wings the owl swoops low
You're welcome to give that a go.
Now climb this tree, give it a try
But with those wings you'll never fly.'

Dilys clambered to the top of the tree and,
just as she reached the top, Olivia Owl flew
away.

There was only one thing for Dilys to do and she
followed Olivia into the air.

Unfortunately Dilys's effort wasn't quite as graceful.
All you could hear was cracking wood as she hit every
branch on her way to the ground.

Well, this wasn't going very well.

Cookie and I helped Dilys to her feet and we quickly hurried along. As we climbed a nearby hill, we watched a beautiful red kite land at the top. When we got there, I told her about Dilys's problem. The red kite replied - but her answer didn't make us feel much better.

'I'm Katie Kite,' she mewed.

'Majestic kites glide in the air.
With those wings I wouldn't dare.
I'm nervous as we're up so high
And it's obvious you'll never fly.'

Katie launched herself into the air and rose gracefully higher and higher.

Dilys now saw her chance to take off as well and ran at full speed down the hill with her wings open wide.

She ran and ran. Faster and faster went her legs - but they stayed firmly on the ground.

A few minutes later she landed with a crash in a bundle at the bottom of the hill.

As we rushed to help Dilys, a colourful puffin landed close by. Looking at the bird, I suddenly had an idea.

He had quite small wings like Dilys, so I was sure he could help.

We pulled Dilys to her feet and went over to the little chap. I explained our situation but I have to be honest and admit he wasn't too helpful.

'I'm Pembroke Puffin,' he squawked.

'My wings are small but fast and strong.
For flying you just look all wrong.
Stay on the ground, forget the sky.
Strange dragon, you will never fly.'

Pembroke started to run and at the same time his little wings went really, really fast. Then he took off and disappeared out to sea and out of sight.

Dilys also started to run, copying him by flapping her wings very fast.

By the time we caught up with her, she was breathless but still very much on the ground. She said she just wanted to go back to her cave.

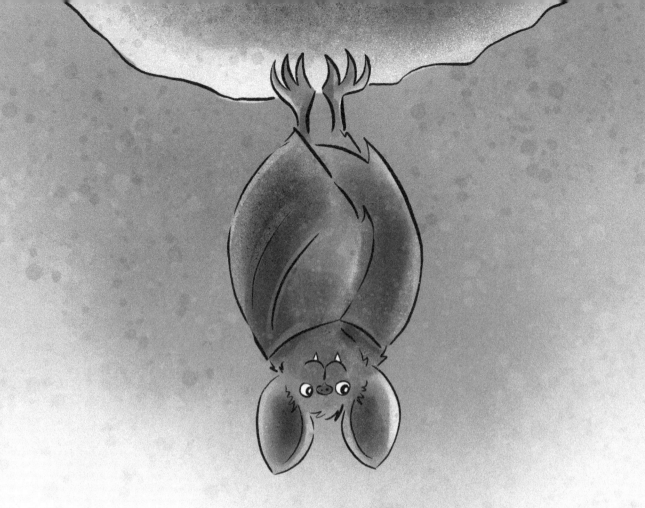

When we got back to the cave, Dilys slumped down on the floor. Suddenly something above me made me look up. There, hanging upside down, was a bat. I decided that we should give this one last try.

'Hello there, Mr Bat,' I said. 'My friend here needs some help to fly. I see you can hang upside down - is that a special trick?'

'I'm Barry Bat,' said the little furry creature very softly. 'When I let go and drop, just like magic I fly. Does she want to give it a go?'

Dilys really didn't want to try. It took a long time to persuade her but eventually she was hanging there, ready to go.

Barry looked across at Dilys and didn't look too convinced. He said,

'In darkness bats can fly the best.
Just taking off will be your test.
Hang upside down, now don't be shy,
Let go - but I don't think you'll fly.'

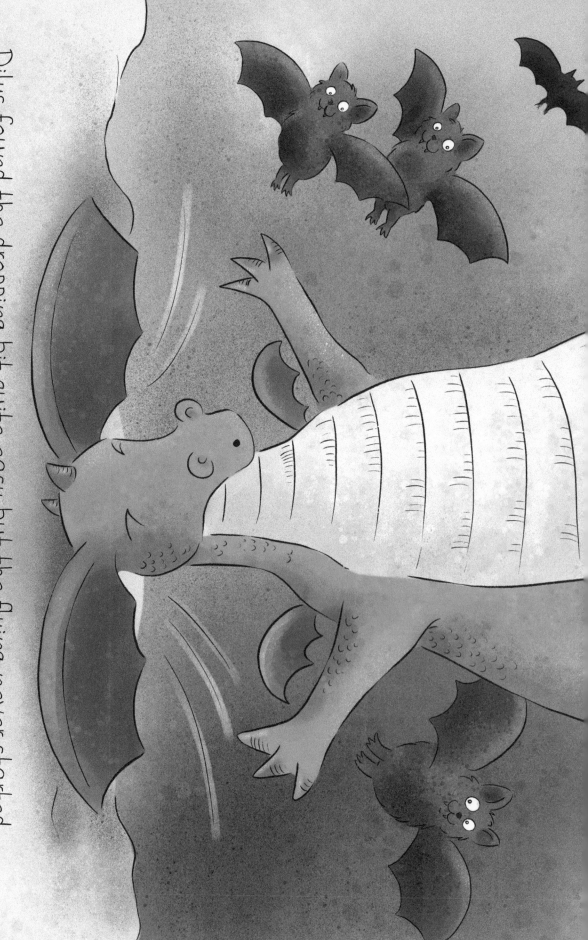

Dilys found the dropping bit quite easy but the flying never started. There was only one thing that was going to happen – and she landed with a heavy crash.

The bat dropped, and flew out of the cave and waited for Dilys.

Dilys said, 'I give up. I'm never going to fly with these wings.'

I had to agree because it seemed like we'd tried everything but then I thought, 'Not with these wings...' Suddenly, I had an idea.

Maybe we had been looking at this all wrong and there was another way. Dilys was a fine-looking dragon. She had small wings but she was magnificent, with a hooge tail and very nice, Spangle-like droopy ears.

I told Dilys that we needed to meet on the beach in the morning.

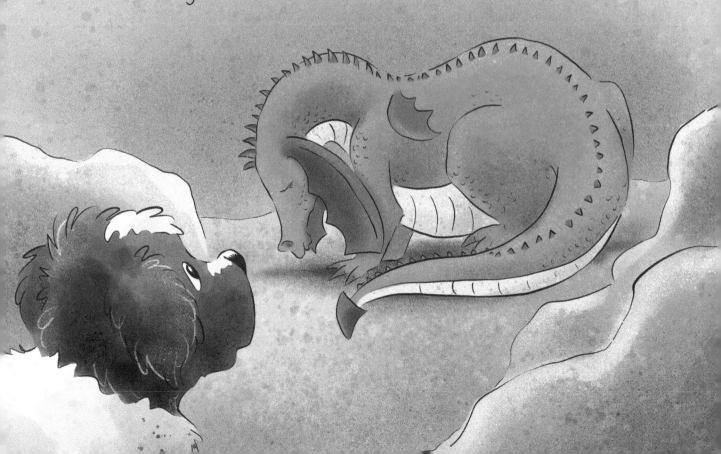

The next morning the Spangles were on the beach and, as usual, they were waiting to chase the ball.

As they ran, they got faster and more excited.

As they did that, their ears began to flap and the Spangles started to lift off. I asked Dilys if she wanted to play and she did.

She had never played with Spangles and she loved it. She ran around and forgot all of her troubles.

Suddenly her ears flapped and she started to fly!

She flew higher and higher and, as she did, her ears went faster and faster. Dilys was flying! She looked down at us and she was so happy.

We may be all quite different,
We don't all look the same.
But if you don't follow what you dream of
It really is a shame.
Anything is possible,
All you have to do is try.
Don't listen when others tell you
That you will never fly...

Cookie and I headed away from the beach. Our work was done - we had helped the Poppit Dragon to fly.

Suddenly Dilys landed in front of us. 'I just wanted to thank you,' she said and she gave us a big hug.

'Now,' said Dilys. 'I just need to learn how to breath fire...'

We ran!

The End

Other books available by the author...

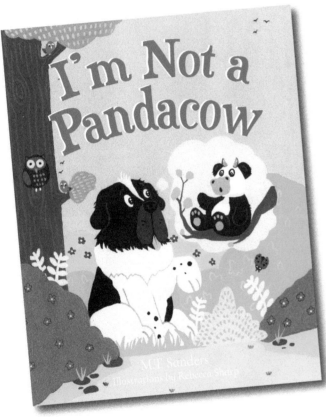

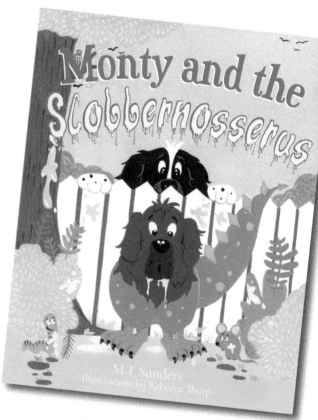

By M.T Sanders

with Illustrations by Rebecca Sharp

ISBN 978-1-912014-7-3

By M.T Sanders

with Illustrations by Rebecca Sharp

ISBN 978-1-912014-79-8

www.montydogge.com

...by the illustrator

Written & Illustrated
by Zoe Saunders

ISBN 978-1-788080-38-5

Written & Illustrated
by Zoe Saunders

ISBN 978-1-789260-88-5

www.whimsicolourart.com

Lightning Source UK Ltd.
Milton Keynes UK
UKHW050808211119
353961UK00003B/7/P